THE PIANO RECITAL

Akiko Miyakoshi

Kids Can Press

Today is Momo's very first piano recital.
She and the other children gather backstage.
"Just play how you've practiced," their
piano teacher says with a smile.

The recital has started.
Momo's heart is racing.
I'll be okay … I'll be okay.
She holds on tightly to her sheet music.

Momo watches the second student walk onstage.

I'll be okay … I'll be okay … Momo repeats in her heart.

"I'll be okay … I'll be okay!"

Oh! Who said that? Looking down, Momo is surprised to see …

A mouseling!
"We're having a recital, too," she says.
"Come watch, Momo."

"But I have to be here," says Momo.
"Don't worry, there's still time until your turn!" says the mouseling, tugging on Momo's tights.

Momo follows her to a small open door at the side of
the stage.

"This way ... this way," the mouseling calls as she
scurries farther and farther inside.

Crouching down, Momo takes a breath and wriggles
through the door ...

A mouse steps onto the stage.

"Ladies and gentlemen, boys and girls, spectators and performers — let us all enjoy today's performances!"

The audience claps.

The curtain rises, and a circus act begins.
Momo watches in awe.

For their finale, the circus performs a towering mouse pyramid. Sprinting across the stage, the last acrobat leaps right to the very top. Momo claps excitedly. "Wow!"

The next performance is a magic act. As the orchestra
plays, a pair of mice dances. Then a scarf is thrown over
the mouse in the red dress, and …

… in the blink of an eye, her dress turns yellow!
"Amazing!" The audience is delighted.

As the dancing mice twirl round and round, the dress changes from one color to another.

Round and round they twirl, faster and faster, until finally, the lady mouse turns into a delicate white butterfly. "Bravo!" the spectators cheer.

The mouse orchestra conductor bows to the
audience and begins the third performance.
    As everyone falls under the spell of the
music, a spotlight shines on a mouse in the
audience, and she begins to sing.

Then a whole chorus of singing and dancing mice fills the stage. Some are small, others tall, some thin, others round. They aren't keeping time with the orchestra, but every mouse seems to be having fun. Momo and the mouseling look at each other and giggle.

The spotlight finds the next performer, a ballerina.
*Mice have such short arms and legs. They look so funny
when they dance*, thinks Momo. But the ballerina moves
gracefully, holding her head high.

Taking hold of a string that hangs from
the ceiling, the ballerina leaps off the stage.
But the moment she soars over the audience,
the string comes loose, and the ballerina
tumbles head over tail …

And lands in Momo's lap!
With a quick hop to her feet, the
ballerina curtsies.
Momo can't help but laugh.

Momo hears a small squeak by her side.

"I'll be okay … I'll be okay …" The mouseling looks up anxiously at Momo. "What if I don't sing well?"

"You'll be okay," Momo reassures her. "I'll go with you onstage."

The mouseling's face lights up.

Momo's own racing heart and worries are long forgotten.

Momo plays the piano while the mouseling sings along. They make such a wonderful duo that everyone in the audience gets up to dance. And then the orchestra and all of the other performers join in, too.

When the piece comes to an end, Momo stands to take a bow. But she sees that she isn't at the mouse recital — she's at her own piano recital! The sound of applause fills the room.

Momo smiles happily. She thinks she hears
the mice clapping, too.

This edition published by Kids Can Press in 2019

First published in Japan in 2012 by Bronze Publishing Inc., Tokyo, under the title *Piano Happyoukai*
Copyright © 2012 Akiko Miyakoshi
English translation rights arranged with Bronze Publishing Inc.
English translation © 2019 Kids Can Press

Kids Can Press gratefully acknowledges the financial support of the Government of Ontario, through Ontario Creates.

Published in Canada and the U.S. by Kids Can Press Ltd.
25 Dockside Drive, Toronto, ON M5A 0B5

Kids Can Press is a Corus Entertainment Inc. company

www.kidscanpress.com

The artwork in this book was rendered in pencil, charcoal and acrylic gouache.
The text is set in Minion Pro.

English edition edited by Yvette Ghione

Printed and bound in Malaysia in 1/2019 by Tien Wah Press (Pte.) Ltd.

CM 19 0 9 8 7 6 5 4 3 2 1

Library and Archives Canada Cataloguing in Publication

Miyakoshi, Akiko, 1982–
[Piano happyoukai. English]
    The piano recital / Akiko Miyakoshi.

Translation of: Piano happyoukai.
ISBN 978-1-5253-0257-2 (hardcover)

    I. Title. II. Title: Piano happyoukai. English.

PZ7.M682Pi 2019   j895.6'36   C2018-906439-0